THIS CANDLEWICK BOOK BELONGS TO:

_____

_____

_____

_____

For Sophie
M. W.
For Felix
L. H.

Text copyright © 1997 by Martin Waddell
Illustrations copyright © 1997 by Leo Hartas

First U.S. edition 1997

Library of Congress Cataloging-in-Publication Data

Waddell, Martin.
Mimi's Christmas / Martin Waddell ; illustrated by Leo Hartas.
—1st U.S. ed.
p.   cm.
Summary: As a mouse family prepares to celebrate Christmas,
its youngest member asks his oldest sister for a special favor.
ISBN 0-7636-0413-5
[1. Christmas—Fiction. 2. Mice—Fiction.] I. Hartas, Leo, ill. II. Title.
PZ7.W1137M1   1997
[E]—dc21   97-6760

2 4 6 8 10 9 7 5 3

Printed in Hong Kong

This book was typeset in Garamond.
The pictures were done in pen and ink and watercolor.

Candlewick Press
2067 Massachusetts Avenue
Cambridge, Massachusetts 02140

Mimi's Christmas

MARTIN WADDELL

illustrated by
LEO HARTAS

CANDLEWICK PRESS
CAMBRIDGE, MASSACHUSETTS

Mimi lived with her mouse sisters and
brothers beneath the big tree.

"Santa Mouse will come soon," Mimi told her
mouse sisters and brothers, as they huddled
up close to the fire. "You must write your
Santa Mouse notes, so he will know what
to put in your stockings."

The mouse brothers and sisters started
scribbling their Santa Mouse notes.

They scribbled . . .

and they scribbled . . .

and they scribbled . . .

and they scribbled . . .

and they scribbled.

"I can't write Santa's note by myself, I'm too small!" Hugo told Mimi.

"I'll do it for you," said Mimi. "Tell me what to write."

This is the note Mimi wrote.

Dear Santa Mouse,
I hope you are well.
I'd like a BIG drum.
Love from
Hugo Mouse
X
P.S. I'm the small one.

"Does Santa Mouse have drums?" asked Hugo,
when they were hanging the lights on their
very own mouse Christmas tree.
"Well, he might have a small one," said Mimi.
"It has to fit in your stocking."
"A small drum that makes a big BOOM
when you bang it?" said Hugo.
"Just wait and see, Hugo," said Mimi.

Christmas Eve came and it snowed.
The mice tumbled and jumbled about
in the snow.

They tumbled . . .

and they jumbled . . .

and they tumbled . . .

and they jumbled . . .

till they all looked like little white mice!

"Supper!" called Mimi, and her mouse
sisters and brothers came in from the
snow. Huddled close to the fire, they
had a Christmas Eve feast with mouse
lemonade and mouse cake.

"Let's leave Santa Mouse some,"
Mimi said, and she put mouse cake and
mouse lemonade out for Santa, under the
mouse Christmas tree in her garden.

"Time for bed, sleepyhead!" Mimi said.
Hugo hung up his mouse stocking at the
end of his little mouse bed. It was a very big
stocking, though he was a very small mouse.
"Is it big enough for my drum?"
Hugo asked.
"Just wait and see, Hugo,"
said Mimi.

The mouse sisters and brothers dreamed of
the toys Santa Mouse would bring for their
mouse stockings.

They dreamed . . .

and they dreamed . . .

and they dreamed . . .

and they dreamed . . .   and they dreamed.

All of them dreamed except Hugo. Hugo was such a small mouse that he felt too excited to sleep. He got out of bed and he looked, but there wasn't a drum in his stocking.

Hugo went looking for Mimi. "I can't get to sleep and that means Santa Mouse won't come," Hugo told Mimi, and he started to cry. "There won't be a drum in my stocking!"

Mimi took Hugo out to the garden.
"Santa Mouse always comes," Mimi said.
"He comes when our mouse world's asleep.
That's how Santa Mouse works."

Mimi put Hugo to bed. And the next
morning . . .

BOOM! BOOM! BOOM!
"Hugo's got his drum," Mimi's mouse
sisters and brothers told Mimi. And . . .

Christmas was noisy at Mimi's!

MARTIN WADDELL is one of the most popular and successful children's writers of his time. He has written many books for children, including *Can't You Sleep, Little Bear?*; *Let's Go Home, Little Bear*; *You and Me, Little Bear*; *Farmer Duck*; *Owl Babies*; *The Big Big Sea*; and *When the Teddy Bears Came*.

LEO HARTAS is the illustrator of numerous books for children, including Martin Waddell's first story about Mimi and her many brothers and sisters, *Mimi's Dream House*.